WHEN MAMA GETS HOME

Marisabina Russo

Greenwillow Books, New York

In loving memory of my mother,
Sabina Wedgewood

Gouache paints were used for the full-color art.
The text type is Geometric 706 Medium.

Printed in Hong Kong by South China Printing
Company (1988) Ltd.
First Edition   10 9 8 7 6 5 4 3 2 1

Library of Congress
Cataloging-in-Publication Data

Russo, Marisabina.
When mama gets home / by Marisabina Russo.
    p.   cm.
Summary: As she helps her older sister and
brother get dinner started, a young girl looks
forward to spending time with her mother
when she gets home from work.
ISBN 0-688-14985-5 (trade).
ISBN 0-688-14986-3 (lib. bdg.)
[1. Working mothers—Fiction.
2. Mother and child—Fiction.
3. Single-parent family—Fiction.]
I. Title.   PZ7.R9192We   1998
[E]—dc21   96-46617   CIP   AC

At five o'clock the telephone rings.
It's Mama! She is getting ready to leave work
and ride the train home to me. To me, my sister,
and my brother.

We have chores to do before Mama gets home.
My sister puts a pot of water on the stove. She
does the cooking because she is the oldest.

My brother peels the carrots. He gets to use
the knife because he is the second oldest.
I set the table.

My sister washes the chicken and pats it dry.
My brother washes the lettuce.
I fold the napkins into little crowns the way
Mama taught me.

When I am done, I stand by the window and look down at the street.
It is getting dark. There are people hurrying back and forth on the sidewalk below.

Mamas with briefcases.

Mamas with shopping bags.

Mamas with backpacks.

Daddies with briefcases.

Daddies with newspapers.

Daddies with brown paper bags of food.

I can't wait for Mama to get home! I have so much to tell her about my day. About the song we learned in music. About the story the teacher read to us. About how I got a star on my report. About how I lost my red pencil case.

When Mama walks in the door, I will jump up and hug her tight. I will rub my face in her soft brown coat.

She will say, "Oh, hello, my little peach!" and hug me back.

The clock ticks and tocks.

It feels like forever, but then I hear Mama's key in the lock.

"Hello, I'm home!" Mama calls out.
I rush to her and hug her until she says,
"My little peach, let me take off my coat
and shoes."

"Mama, you need to sign this for school," says my sister.

"Mama, I need to talk to you about my math teacher," says my brother.

"Mama, I want to sing the new song I learned, and anyway I was first!" I say.

Mama tells us to hold our horses. She needs to hang up her coat and put on her slippers and finish making dinner.

When we sit down to eat, everyone starts talking at the same time.

Mama quiets us down.
"One at a time," she says.

My sister goes first. She always gets to go
first. She goes on and on about high school.
Blah blah blah.
Then it is my brother's turn. He goes on and
on about his basketball team.
Blah blah blah.

Finally it is my turn. I tell Mama everything.
"Sounds like a busy day," says Mama.

After dinner Mama starts a bath for me.

The telephone rings.

My sister calls out, "Mama, it's for you!"

I play with my sponges and listen to Mama.
She's talking to Grandma.

When I step out of the tub, Mama is there to wrap me in a warm, fluffy towel. She rubs my hair with another towel. She tells me to brush my teeth.

I get under the covers with my teddy and
my doll. Mama sits beside me. Finally I have
Mama all to myself!
She reads a book to me, the one I picked out
at the school library today.

Mama gives me a kiss.

I give her a kiss back.

When she turns out the light, she sits on my
bed for a while. We talk in the dark until
Mama says, "It's time for you to go to sleep,
my little peach. Good night, sweet dreams..."

good night."